OTHER BOOKS BY QUENTIN BLAKE

Mrs Armitage on Wheels
Mrs Armitage and the Big Wave
The Story of the Dancing Frog
Nursery Rhyme Book
Fantastic Daisy Artichoke
The Green Ship
All Join In
Clown
Cockatoos
Simpkin
Zagazoo

A Red Fox Book

Published by Random House Children's Books
20 Vauxhall Bridge Road, London SW1V 2SA
A division of Random House UK Ltd
London Melbourne Sydney Auckland
Johannesburg and agencies throughout the world

copyright © Quentin Blake 1980

7 9 10 8

First published in Great Britain by Jonathan Cape Ltd 1980
Red Fox Edition 1999

Printed in Hong Kong

RANDOM HOUSE UK Limited Reg. No. 954009
ISBN 0 09 940042 1

Mr Magnolia has only one boot.

He has an old trumpet

that goes rooty-toot —

And two lovely sisters
who play on the flute —

But Mr Magnolia has only one boot.

In his pond live a frog

and a toad and a newt —

He has green parakeets

who pick holes in his suit —

And some very fat owls
who are learning to hoot —
But Mr Magnolia
has only one boot.

He gives rides to his friends

when he goes for a scoot —

And the splash is immense
when he comes down
the chute —

But Mr Magnolia
has only one boot.

Just look at the way that

he juggles with fruit!

The mice all march past

as he takes the salute!

And his dinosaur!

What a MAGNIFICENT

brute!

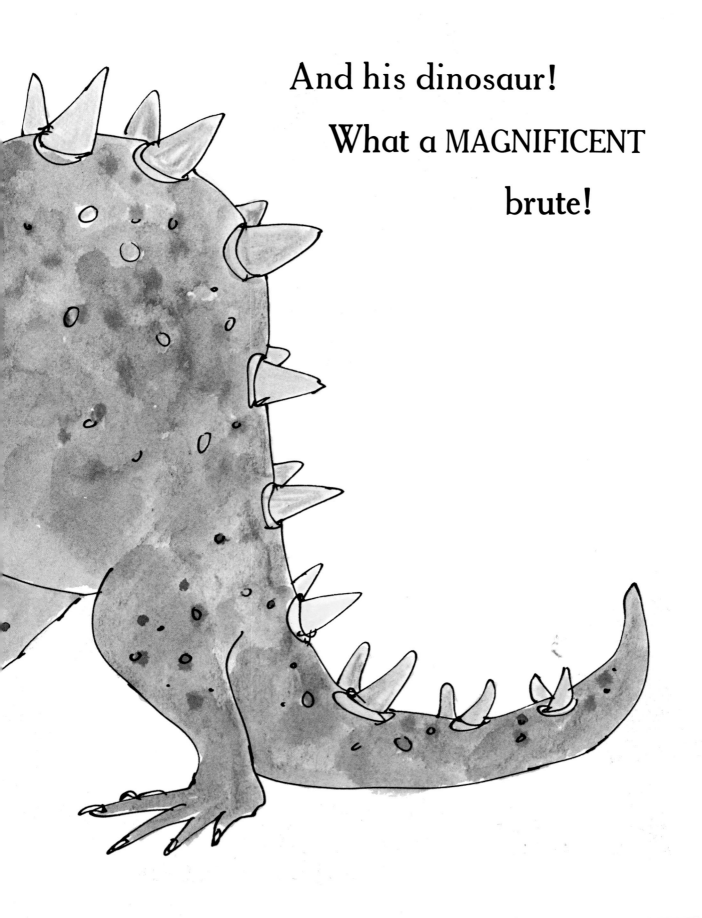

But Mr Magnolia —
poor Mr Magnolia!
— Mr Magnolia
has
only one boot . . .

Hey —

Wait a minute . . .

Now then . . .

Keep going . . .

What's this?

Look!

It's a boot!

It's a boot!

Whoopee
for Mr Magnolia's
new boot!

Good night.